Amazing Mallika

Written by **Jami Parkison**

Illustrated by **Itoko Maeno**

MarshMedia, Kansas City, Missouri

For Kate and Gabriel — J.P.

For C.T. — I.M.

Special thanks to Tina Laughlin,
Margaret and Clayton Marsh, Mike Nichols,
and Jeannie Wilkerson

First Printing 1997
Second Printing 1999

Text ©1997 by Marsh Film Enterprises, Inc.
Illustrations ©1997 by Itoko Maeno

All rights reserved. No part of this book may be reproduced in any form
without permission in writing from Marsh Film Enterprises, Inc., P. O.
Box 8082, Shawnee Mission, Kansas 66208, USA, except by a newspaper
or magazine reviewer who wishes to quote brief passages in a review.

Published by **MARSH**media

A Division of Marsh Film Enterprises, Inc.
P. O. Box 8082
Shawnee Mission, KS 66208

Library of Congress Cataloging-in-Publication Data

Parkison, Jami.
  Amazing Mallika/written by Jami Parkison; illustrated by Itoko Maeno.
     p. cm.
  Summary: A tiger cub who lives in India's Ranthambhore Park wildlife
preserve learns some ways to control her quick temper. Endpages give
factual information about India.
   ISBN 1-55942-087-1
  [1. Temper—Fiction. 2. Anger—Fiction. 3. Tigers—Fiction.
4. India—Fiction.] I. Maeno, Itoko, ill. II. Title.
PZ7.P2394Am 1997   96-9571
[Fic]—dc20

Book layout and typography by Cirrus Design

Printed in Hong Kong

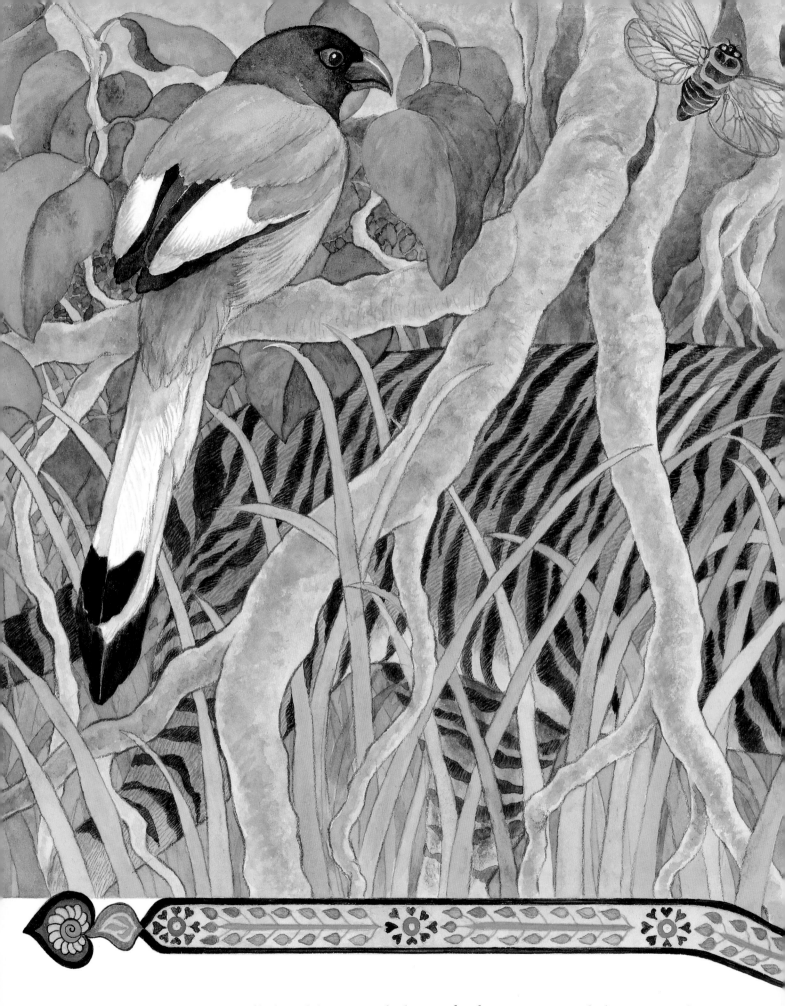

Morning sunlight shimmered through the canopy of the sweeping banyan tree. The air hummed with the sounds of Ranthambhore Park: cicadas sang, tree-pies chattered, and langur monkeys squealed.

The ruins of palaces, pavilions, and watchtowers marked the site where princes once ruled, but now the park belonged to the animals. Most of all it belonged to the tigers.

Mallika and her brother, Ben, had come with their mother, Babur, to the lake. A thin line of grass hid the cats from animals stopping for a drink. The tigress was teaching her cubs to hunt.

"Hush now," said Babur. "Wait. Be calm."

Being calm was hard for Mallika. She was a hot-tempered little tiger.

For two days the cubs hid with their mother behind the grass. Not a tail or whisker flicked. Jackal and spotted deer came and went. Sambar fed at the water's edge, lifted their heads warily, then sprang away.

"Too far," whispered Babur.

But on the third day, the waiting ended.

A peacock strolled by the grassy hideout.
In an instant Mallika leaped at the startled bird.
"Ieeee, ieeee," it cried.
Mallika pounced, just as she'd seen Babur do, and snatched the darting bird.

The peacock spread its wings, covering Mallika's eyes. Blinded, Mallika stumbled into a bush, then backed into the banyan trunk. She was about to pin the thrashing peacock to the ground when Ben jumped forward and grabbed it.

"It's mine," Mallika snarled. Babur had warned Mallika about her quick temper, but what could Mallika do? Ben was trying to take her peacock, and that made her furious.

Both cubs tugged at the bird. Mallika hissed at Ben. She tried to push him into a thicket full of burrs, but in the confusion of feathers and paws, Mallika ended up rolling into the thicket herself.

"Ieee, ieeee," cried the peacock as it fluttered to safety in the banyan.

Covered with burrs, Mallika glared at her brother. She was about to pounce on him again when Babur stepped between the two cubs.

"He tried to steal the peacock," Mallika said to her mother. "He makes me soooo mad."

"True, your brother didn't play fair," said Babur, "but nobody wins when you lose your temper. No one has the peacock now. When you are really mad, you need to find another way to let off steam."

Mallika stomped angrily in a little circle, mumbling under her breath, "The peacock is gone, and I'm covered with burrs, all because —." Around and around she marched. "All because — I was too hot headed," she finally realized.

12

Amazingly, marching had made Mallika feel better. Her anger had melted. "I'll never get so angry again," she promised. "No matter what!"
But that was before the langur monkeys laughed at her.

The midday sun hung high overhead. Flies buzzed over the parched grass, and water bugs skated across the lake. Mallika spent the morning trying to clean the burrs from her fur. She licked. She rolled in the dirt. She rubbed against the banyan tree.

"What a mess!" she said.

High in the banyan, the monkeys jeered, "Malli's a mess. Malli's a mess. Hee-hee-hee."

The white dots on Mallika's ears twitched. What did those monkeys say?

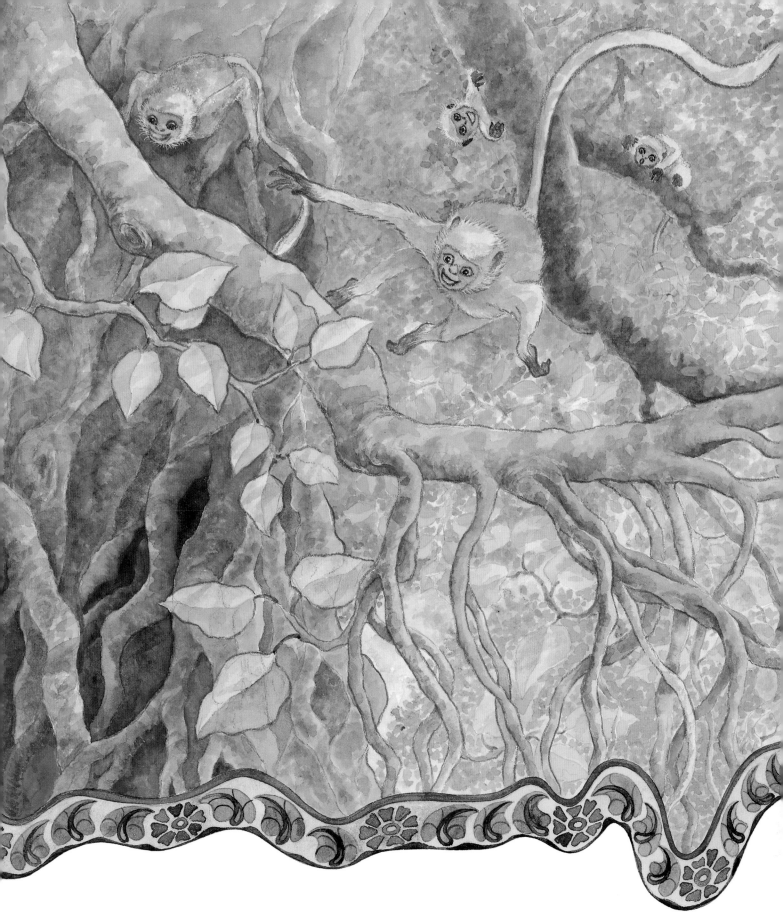

"Burrs, burrs, burrs in her fur," the monkeys chanted.

Mallika curled her lip and growled.

"Malli's a mess with burrs in her fur," the monkeys mocked.

"Those monkeys make me soooo mad," she said, her yellow-green eyes burning.

"Soooo mad," the monkeys taunted. "Soooo mad. Malli's mad. Malli's mad. Hee-hee-hee."

That did it. Mallika lost her temper again. In a ball of fury, she shot up the tree. "I'll show them!"

Higher and higher she climbed. Through the leaves she saw the monkeys' grinning faces and curving tails.

Sitting coolly on the tip of a branch, one monkey twittered, "Malli's mad. Malli's mad. Hee-hee-hee."

Mallika crawled out on a tiny limb. The monkey swung to a higher branch. How tricky — how annoying! Mallika inched forward, hoping to snag the long tail.

When she looked down, Mallika saw that Babur was watching.

"You're too short tempered for your own good," her mother said.

"But these monkeys are mean. They make me soooo mad."

"It's best to ignore someone who is mean. Walk away. Do something else, something you like to do."

Mallika thought for a moment.

Suddenly, Mallika scrambled from the tree and ran toward the lake. In a bounding leap, she sailed through the air and landed — plop — in the water. She splashed for a while and then stretched out at the lake's edge.

Amazingly, the clatter of the monkeys and the heat of the anger faded away.

Being angry wasn't any fun. Mallika really liked being calm. Once again she decided never to let herself become so mad. "No matter what!"

In the late afternoon, as the sun set, the sky turned scarlet. Mallika was
resting on a rock, drying her fur. All at once, a beetle ran from under a leaf.
The cub jumped up and chased the bug as it scurried
    around the pool,
        up a broken column,
            and along a crumbling wall.

Mallika stepped carefully along the edge of the wall toward the beetle. Halfway across, the little tiger lost her balance. She tried to catch herself, to hook a claw over the edge, but instead she tumbled into a dark chamber, the underground room of an ancient temple.

A dazed Mallika wiped the spider webs from her eyes. The stone wall towered overhead like a rocky cliff.

Mallika tried to leap out, but the wall was too high. She tried to claw her way up, but the sides were too steep. She scratched furiously in the dirt, but that didn't help at all.

Mallika glared up at the full yellow moon and the deep blue shadows spreading over the ruins. "How could I be so clumsy?" she roared. "And how will I ever get out of this hole?"

Mallika was just too angry — too angry with herself — to think clearly. She made one last lunge at the wall, then collapsed in a jumbled heap.

When Mallika opened her eyes, the morning sun shimmered once more through the leaves of the banyan tree.

Still trapped.

"How will I ever climb out?" she wondered. One thing was certain: Mallika had to stay calm. "I'm NOT going to lose my temper again," she said.

Mallika looked around the chamber. For the first time, she noticed a tangle of vines in the corner. A perfect step ladder. Amazing!

Mallika raised a paw into the vines. "Ouch!" she said. The vines were full of thorns. A low growl started to rumble from Mallika's throat, but she stopped herself. "Stay calm!" she said. And with that, Mallika began to climb up the vines. Before long she was nearly to the top. And not once

— not when the leaves tickled her ears

— not when the thorns poked her paws

— not even when the monkeys, overhead in the banyan, began to cackle, "Mallika, Mallika, Mallika —"

— not once did Mallika lose her temper.

As the little tiger pulled herself to the top of the wall, Babur ran up the broken column. "I've been searching everywhere," she said and nuzzled the cub. "The monkeys found you. They told me where to look."

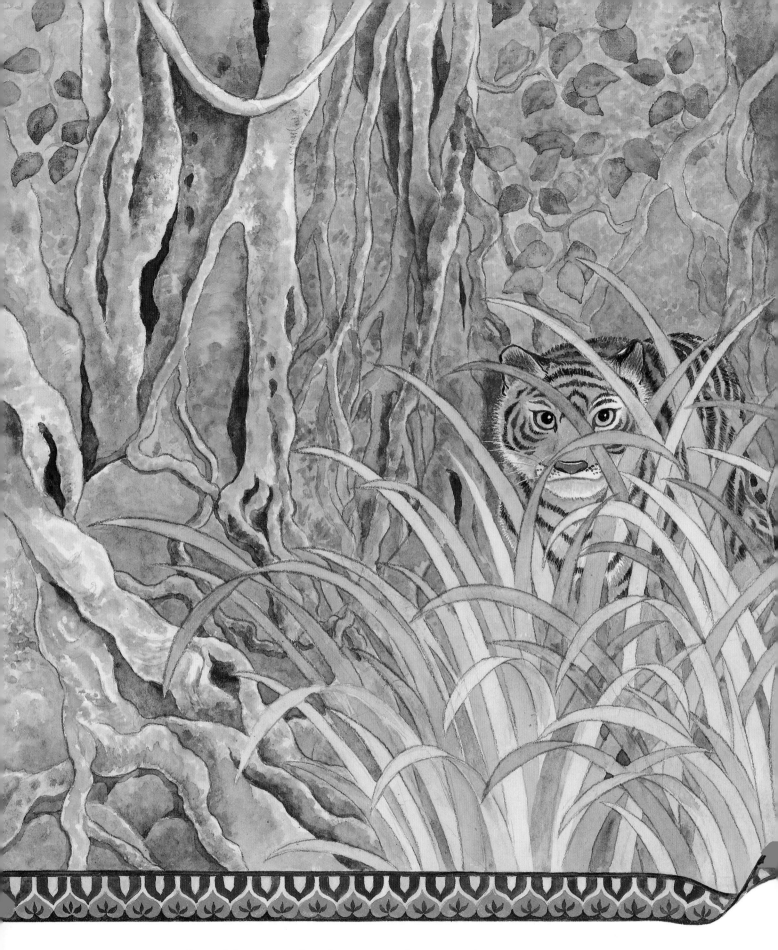

In Ranthambhore Park, the green leaves of the banyan drooped under the blaze of the noonday sun. Purple water lilies faded in the heat. Only the red and yellow tigers sparkled like jewels inside the thin line of grass. Babur and her cubs were once again waiting for thirsty animals to visit the watering place.

All day long they waited. Quietly. Calmly. For Mallika, being calm was still hard, but she had finally learned that losing her temper didn't make things better.

And so, even though her paws were tender from the thorny vines and even though Ben chased a peahen all by himself, Mallika still didn't get mad.

And that's not all — high in the banyan tree, the monkeys were chanting something they had never chanted before.

Mallika, who had once been such a hot-tempered little tiger, was just sure they were saying, "Malli's amazing. Malli's amazing. Hee-hee-hee."

And, you know, they probably were.

Dear Parents and Educators:

Learning to identify, accept, and express our emotions is an ongoing process for all of us as human beings. Handling a powerful emotion like anger is difficult for many of us and is especially challenging for children.

Many adults are uncomfortable with their own feelings of anger and feel inadequate to deal with this emotion in children. Too often we ask children to falsify their feelings. "Take that frown off your face!" we say, requiring a child to deny his true emotions and to play-act insincere ones. It is important that children learn to recognize and accept their own feelings of anger. Only then can they learn positive ways to express those feelings.

Caring adults need to take time with children to teach strategies for anger management. We need to assure children that the sometimes frightening "out of control" feelings that anger involves are in fact quite controllable through careful thinking and positive behavior choices. As children identify their personal strategies for success, they will gain enthusiasm and self-confidence, and they'll be on their way to adopting a healthier lifestyle.

The story of Mallika helps children understand that anger is a normal emotion, but that losing one's temper can only lead to more trouble. Mallika's mother offers her daughter some helpful ways to respond to feelings of anger, and Mallika learns to make choices that lead to more positive results. She is also able to recognize that other people are not responsible for her behavior. She has the power to choose her attitude and to overcome difficulties.

To help youngsters better understand the message of *Amazing Mallika*, discuss the following questions with them:

- How did Mallika feel when her brother tried to take her peacock?
- What did she do about it?
- Did her actions make her happy?
- When in the story did Mallika get angry again?
- What did she choose to do? Did it help?
- What strategies did Mallika's mother suggest?
- When do you feel angry?
- Who chooses your behavior?
- How do you solve problems without hurting yourself or others?
- How do you feel about yourself when you control your temper?

Here are some ways you can help young people learn to control their anger and problem solve effectively:

- Validate children's feelings. Help them to name different feelings.
- Assure children that anger is an emotion that all of us feel.
- Share tension relieving strategies that work for you.
- Teach children that disagreements between individuals are a normal part of life. We don't all think alike!
- Set up and enforce classroom or family rules for showing respect with words and actions.
- Look for your child's successes in managing his or her anger.

Available from MarshMedia

Storybooks — Hardcover with dust jacket and full-color illustrations throughout.

Videos — The original story and illustrations combined with dramatic narration, music, and sound effects.

Activity Books — Softcover collections of games, puzzles, maps, and project ideas designed for each title.

Amazing Mallika, written by Jami Parkison, illustrated by Itoko Maeno. 32 pages. ISBN 1-55942-087-1. Video. 15:05 run time. ISBN 1-55942-088-X.

Bailey's Birthday, written by Elizabeth Happy, illustrated by Andra Chase. 32 pages. ISBN 1-55942-059-6. Video. 18:00 run time. ISBN 1-55942-060-X.

Bea's Own Good, written by Linda Talley, illustrated by Andra Chase. 32 pages. ISBN 1-55942-092-8. Video. 15:00 run time. ISBN 1-55942-093-6.

Clarissa, written by Carol Talley, illustrated by Itoko Maeno. 32 pages. ISBN 1-55942-014-6. Video. 13:00 run time. ISBN 1-55942-023-5.

Gumbo Goes Downtown, written by Carol Talley, illustrated by Itoko Maeno. 32 pages. ISBN 1-55942-042-1. Video. 18:00 run time. ISBN 1-55942-043-X.

Hana's Year, written by Carol Talley, illustrated by Itoko Maeno. 32 pages. ISBN 1-55942-034-0. Video. 17:10 run time. ISBN 1-55942-035-9.

Inger's Promise, written by Jami Parkison, illustrated by Andra Chase. 32 pages. ISBN 1-55942-080-4. Video. 15:00 run time. ISBN 1-55942-081-2.

Jackson's Plan, written by Linda Talley, illustrated by Andra Chase. 32 pages. ISBN 1-55942-104-5. Video. 15:00 run time. ISBN 1-55942-105-3.

Jomo and Mata, written by Alyssa Chase, illustrated by Andra Chase. 32 pages. ISBN 1-55942-051-0. Video. 20:00 run time. ISBN 1-55942-052-9.

Kiki and the Cuckoo, written by Elizabeth Happy, illustrated by Andra Chase. 32 pages. ISBN 1-55942-038-3. Video. 14:30 run time. ISBN 1-55942-039-1.

Kylie's Concert, written by Patty Sheehan, illustrated by Itoko Maeno. 32 pages. ISBN 1-55942-046-4. Video. 17:20 run time. ISBN 1-55942-047-2.

Kylie's Song, written by Patty Sheehan, illustrated by Itoko Maeno. 32 pages. (Advocacy Press) ISBN 0-911655-19-0. Video. 12:00 run time. ISBN 1-55942-021-9.

Minou, written by Mindy Bingham, illustrated by Itoko Maeno. 64 pages. (Advocacy Press) ISBN 0-911655-36-0. Video. 18:30 run time. ISBN 1-55942-015-4.

Molly's Magic, written by Penelope Colville Paine, illustrated by Itoko Maeno. 32 pages. ISBN 1-55942-068-5. Video. 16:00 run time. ISBN 1-55942-069-3.

My Way Sally, written by Mindy Bingham and Penelope Paine, illustrated by Itoko Maeno. 48 pages. (Advocacy Press) ISBN 0-911655-27-1. Video. 19:30 run time. ISBN 1-55942-017-0.

Papa Piccolo, written by Carol Talley, illustrated by Itoko Maeno. 32 pages. ISBN 1-55942-028-6. Video. 18:00 run time. ISBN 1-55942-029-4.

Pequeña the Burro, written by Jami Parkison, illustrated by Itoko Maeno. 32 pages. ISBN 1-55942-055-3. Video. 14:00 run time. ISBN 1-55942-056-1.

Plato's Journey, written by Linda Talley, illustrated by Itoko Maeno. 32 pages. ISBN 1-55942-100-2. Video. 15:00 run time. ISBN 1-55942-101-0.

Tessa on Her Own, written by Alyssa Chase, illustrated by Itoko Maeno. 32 pages. ISBN 1-55942-064-2. Video. 14:00 run time. ISBN 1-55942-065-0.

Thank You, Meiling, written by Linda Talley, illustrated by Itoko Maeno. 32 pages. ISBN 1-55942-118-5. Video. 15:00 run time. ISBN 1-55942-119-3.

Time for Horatio, written by Penelope Paine, illustrated by Itoko Maeno. 48 pages. (Advocacy Press) ISBN 0-911655-33-6. Video. 19:00 run time. ISBN 1-55942-026-X.

Tonia the Tree, written by Sandy Stryker, illustrated by Itoko Maeno. 32 pages. (Advocacy Press) ISBN 0-911655-16-6. Video. 12:10 run time. ISBN 1-55942-019-7.

You can find storybooks at better bookstores. Or you may order storybooks, videos, and activity books direct by calling MarshMedia toll free at 1-800-821-3303.

MarshMedia has been publishing high-quality, award-winning learning materials for children since 1969. To receive a free catalog, call 1-800-821-3303, or visit us at www.marshmedia.com.

INDIA

India is a country located in southern Asia. Its capital is New Delhi. One of the largest and most geographically diverse countries, India's landscape includes mountain ranges, fertile farmlands, deserts, and lush forests. At one time, most of India was governed by Great Britain. In 1947 Great Britain granted India independence following a nonviolent movement led by Mohandas Gandhi — the *Mahatma*. The country is now made up of twenty-five states. Mallika's story takes place in the state of Rajasthan, known for the brilliantly colored cotton cloth woven and dyed there.

INDIA'S PEOPLE

India has more people than any other country except China. Both Hindi and English are recognized as official national languages. Thirteen other regional languages are officially recognized. Many religions are practiced in India, including Hinduism, Jainism, Buddhism, Islam, Sikhism and Christianity. In this land of cultural and geographical diversity, clothing styles — the way a woman's sari is worn or the way a man drapes his turban — often indicate the region from which a person comes.

SAMBAR

The sambar, India's largest deer, can often be seen partially submerged in the lakes of Ranthambhore Park, grazing on water lily leaves and other water vegetation. Often snowy egrets and herons fish from the sambar's back! At Ranthambhore Park the sambar is the tiger's most important prey species.

PEACOCK

The peacock is the national bird of India. The male bird is called a "peacock," and the female is called a "peahen." Thousands of these birds inhabit the forests of Ranthambhore Park. The peacock is known for his brilliant green, blue and turquoise feathers, marked with iridescent "eyes."